Jane R. Howard

WHEN I'M SLEEPY

illustrated by Lynne Cherry

DUTTON CHILDREN'S BOOKS   NEW YORK

Library of Congress Cataloging in Publication Data

Howard, Jane R.
    When I'm sleepy.
    Summary: A child speculates about sleeping in various
places other than one's own, and most desirable, warm bed.
    1. Children's stories, American.   [1.Sleep—Fiction]
I. Cherry, Lynne, ill.   II. Title.
PZ7.H83297W4   1985   [E]   84-25895
ISBN 0-525-44204-9

Published in the United States by
Dutton Children's Books, a division of
Penguin Books USA Inc.

Editor: Ann Durell   Designer: Isabel Warren-Lynch

Printed in Hong Kong by South China Printing Co.
COBE   20 19 18 17 16 15 14 13 12

to my daughter,
Nancy Lenore
J.R.H.

to my dear friends
Rick, Linda, Natalie
and Michael Diamond
L.C.

When I'm sleepy,

sometimes I wish I could curl up in a basket

or fall asleep in a downy nest.

When I'm sleepy, and I stretch and I yawn,

I wonder how it would be to sleep in a swamp

or a hollow log

or crawl into a cozy cave and sleep all winter.

When I'm sleepy, and my eyelids feel heavy,

I wonder how it would be to sleep standing up

or high on a rocky, mountain ledge

or hanging upside down

or perched on the branch of a tree.

When I'm so sleepy that I just keep yawning
and yawning,

I'm glad I don't have to sleep where it's freezing cold.

When I'm sleepy, and my eyelids get so heavy
I can hardly hold them open,

I'm glad I don't have to sleep underwater

or where it's hot and dry.

When I'm sleepy, and my eyelids keep falling shut,

I'm so glad I can go to sleep in my very own bed
under my own warm blanket
with my head on my own soft pillow.